# The
# Halloween
# Adventure

written by Dandi

Katy Cat watched Bitsy and the other witches scurry around the cabin. Tonight was the once-in-a-year night: Halloween!

"Good news, Katy!" shouted Bitsy Witch. "The other witches said you're old enough to ride with me this year!"

Katy Cat purred at the
thought of flying with Bitsy.

"Wait till you see my brand
new broom, Katy!  You'll love it!"
And Bitsy stroked her black cat.

"No fair!" whined Wilmeena, the grouchiest witch in the world. "You get a new broom, and mine's all wrecked!"

Wilmeena had wrecked her broom swatting cats! Katy was terrified of Wilmeena and her wicked cat.

Bitsy kissed her cat on the head. "I have to go pick up my hat," she said. "See you later, Katy Cat."

As soon as Bitsy was gone, Wilmeena grabbed Bitsy's new broom. Then she and her cat crept outside, hiding the broom between them.

Katy Cat followed the evil pair through the woods. From behind a tree, she watched as Wilmeena stuck Bitsy's beautiful new broom in the briars.

"That will fix *her*!" Wilmeena cackled.

Back at the cabin, poor Bitsy was frantic. "Oh, Katy Cat," she cried. "Where did I put it? If I can't find my broom, we'll miss Halloween!"

Katy meowed and meowed. How could she make Bitsy understand?

"Tsk, tsk. Such a shame," cackled Wilmeena. And she and the other witches left for the haunting.

Suddenly Katy had an idea! Back through the woods she ran. When she reached the broom, she jumped aboard, dug in her claws, and flew up, up, up!

"Katy Cat!" Bitsy screeched as her cat wobbled over the cabin. Katy managed to swoop down. Bitsy leaped on in front, and off they flew to catch the others.

Wilmeena was so startled to see Bitsy and Katy, she and her cat fell off their broom into a pile of hay!

"Happy Halloween!" Bitsy yelled down to them.

"Meow Meow-meow!" said Katy Cat – which in cat language means HAPPY HALLOWEEN!